# The Boy Who Ate EVERYTHING

### by Clemency Pearce

**TOP THAT**

Licensed exclusively to Top That Publishing Ltd
Tide Mill Way, Woodbridge, Suffolk, IP12 1AP, UK
www.topthatpublishing.com
Text copyright © 2014 Clemency Pearce
Illustrations copyright © 2014 Tide Mill Media
All rights reserved
2 4 6 8 9 7 5 3 1
Manufactured in China

Illustrated by Richard Watson
Written by Clemency Pearce

ISBN 978-1-78445-373-2

A catalogue record for this book is available from the British Library

*For Theo x*

The most gruesome thing I EVER did was when I was a little kid.

I was SO hungry on that day, I swallowed all that came my way.

I ate some mud,
I ate some ants,

I ate my brother's underpants.

# A TIN OF BEANS!

At last I'd filled my naughty tum ...
then came a grumbling from my BUM!

It felt as though the ground was shaking.
Oh, what noise my gut was making!

# Oh cripes!

A bottom burp so **HUGE** and loud
was shooting me above the clouds!

Flying with such style and grace,

ZOOOOOOOOOOOOOOOOOOMING

nto outer space!

This botty squeak went on and on,
until the Earth was almost gone!

So there I sat all on my own,
in silent orbit far from home.

How the heck would I get down?
And then I heard ANOTHER sound ...

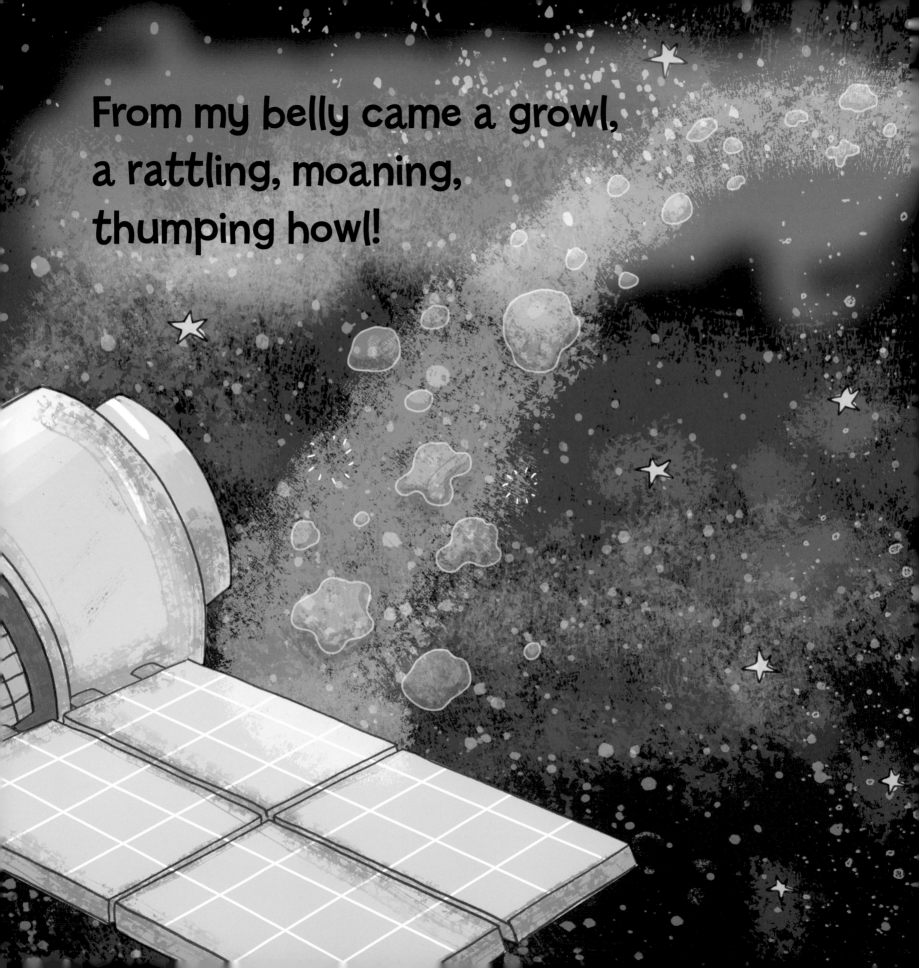

From my belly came a growl,
a rattling, moaning,
thumping howl!

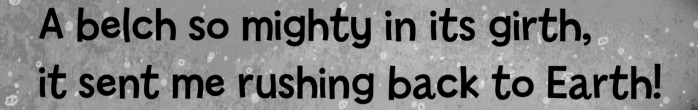

A belch so mighty in its girth,
it sent me rushing back to Earth!

I landed, BUMP,

right on my dad.
My mum was fuming,
steaming mad!

'What a mess!' she cried, in tears.
'You're grounded now for 80 years!'

So please be careful what you eat,
stick to greens and fruit and meat.

Recall the mess beans get you in ...

I think I'll have
another tin ...